Lucy lives at
64 Zoo Lane,
right next door
to the zoo. Every
night, she climbs
out of her window,
slides down the long
long neck of Georgina
the Giraffe and listens to
one of the animals
tell her a story . . .

...and tonight it's the

For Geraldine, Joe, Jack and Jesse
A.V.

ZED THE ZEBRA
written and illustrated by An Vrombaut
Book based on 'The Story of Zed the Zebra' of the TV series
64 Zoo Lane written by An Vrombaut and John Grace.

© Millimages S.A. / Zoo Lane Productions Ltd 2001

British Library Cataloguing in Publication Data
A catalogue record of this book is available from the British Library.

ISBN-13: 978 0 340 79560 6

First edition published 2001
1

Published by Hodder Children's Books
a division of Hachette Children's Books
338 Euston Road London NW1 3BH

Printed in China

This edition published 2007
for Index Books Ltd

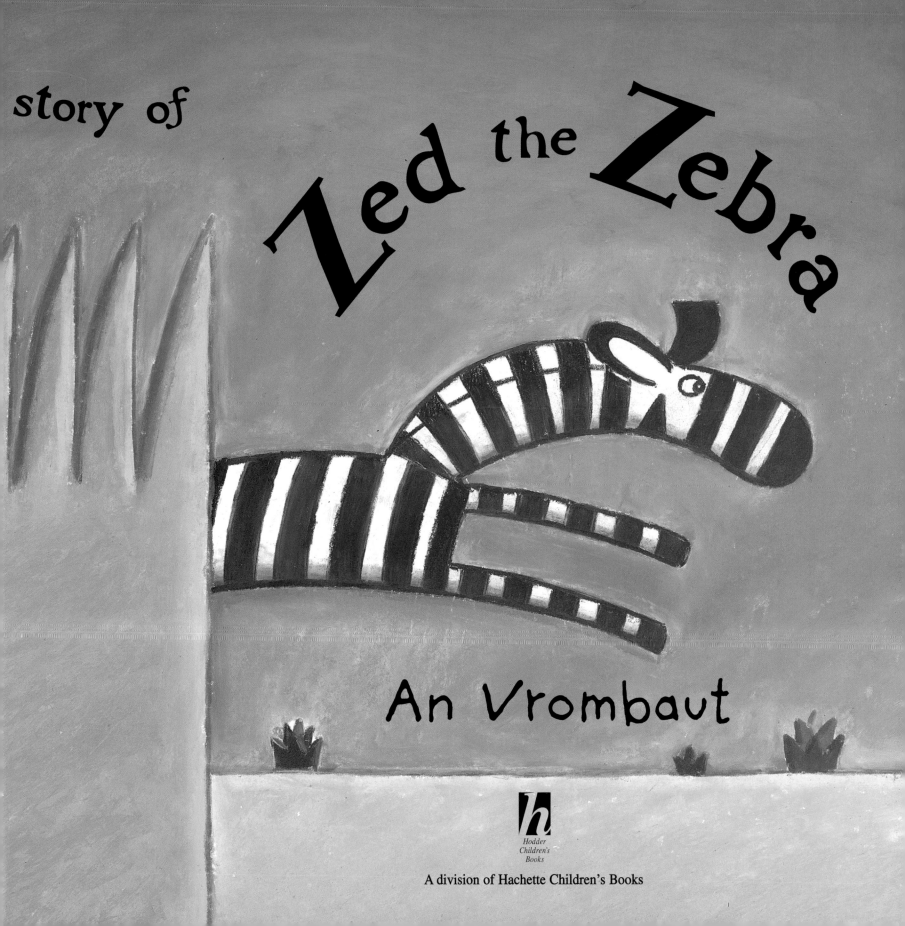

story of

Zed the Zebra

An Vrombaut

Hodder
Children's
Books

A division of Hachette Children's Books

Zed the Zebra was fast, **very fast.**

He could run faster than Ronald the Rhino, faster than Georgina the Giraffe, faster than Herbert the Warthog, and even faster than Nelson the Elephant.

Then one day, the animals
decided to challenge Zed to a race.
'Not just any old race,' explained
Nelson, 'an obstacle race.'
'Obstacle race or not, I'll still
win!' said Zed, as he strutted to
the start line. 'After all, I'm the one
with go-faster-stripes!'

The Snip-snip Bird whistled
the start signal and all
the animals raced
away.

Zed thundered ahead to the first
obstacle – the Jungle.

He jumped this way,
he jumped that way,
but the jungle was so thick that
Zed could not find a way through.

But Nelson the Elephant could!
With his big feet he flattened a path all
the way through the jungle.
'You may have go-faster-stripes,'
trumpeted Nelson to Zed, 'but I'm the one
with **tree-trampling-feet!**'

Zed followed Nelson and raced ahead to the next obstacle – the Big Boulders.

'Piece of cake!' thought Zed. But the Big Boulders were too big and too wobbly for Zed.

But not for Ronald the Rhino!

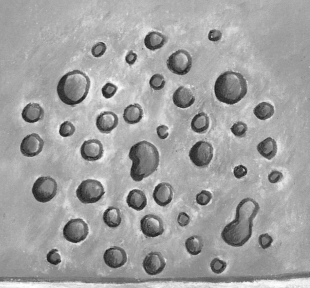

He crushed the Big Boulders into lots and lots of little ones.

'You may have go-faster-stripes,' muttered Ronald to Zed, 'but I'm the one with the **boulder-bashing-horn.**'

Zed soon caught up with Ronald.
'See you at the finish!' he laughed,
as he raced to the next obstacle –
the Great Grasses. But the Great
Grasses were too tall. Zed couldn't
see anything, the way in, or the
way out . . .

But Georgina the Giraffe could!

With her neck she could see over
the Great Grasses and find
her way out.
'You may have go-faster-stripes,'
sang Georgina to Zed, 'but
I'm the one with the

special-stretchy-neck!'

But Zed was still the fastest runner.
He raced away until he came to the last obstacle –
the Blue Mountain.
But the mountain was too steep.
The faster Zed ran, the more he slipped.

How would he get past the Blue Mountain?
He didn't know how to climb . . .

But Herbert the Warthog
knew how to dig!

He started to dig
a long narrow tunnel
to the other side of
the mountain.

'You may have
go-faster-stripes,'
snorted Herbert at Zed,
'but I'm the one with
dig-deeper-claws!'

But Zed wasn't going to be beaten by a warthog!
He raced ahead once more. He had almost reached
the finish when he stopped to admire his reflection
in the waterhole.

'Just look at those go-faster-stripes', said Zed.
'No one can beat me now!'

And then SUDDENLY there was a big

WHOOSH...

. . . and the other
animals raced past Zed.

'The winners are
Georgina,
Nelson,
Ronald
and
Herbert,'

announced the Snip-snip bird.

'. . . and in second place Zed the Zebra!'

'Well . . . I suppose I'm not always the *fastest*,' sighed Zed.
Georgina smiled. 'Sometimes you win and sometimes you lose, but at least we all had *fun*!'

Zed agreed.

'And now it's time for a **party**!'
he said and tapped a few dance
steps. 'By the way, did you know
I'm the best dancer in all of Africa?'